THE WORLD OF
MIXED MARTIAL ARTS

# A NEW GENERATION OF WARRIORS

## THE *HISTORY* OF MIXED MARTIAL ARTS

### BY JIM WHITING

Consultant:
Robert Rousseau
Martial Arts Guide, *About.com*
Senior Writer, *MMAFighting.com*

Velocity is published by Capstone Press,
151 Good Counsel Drive, P.O. Box 669, Mankato, Minnesota 56002.
www.capstonepress.com

Books published by Capstone Press are manufactured with paper containing at least 10 percent post-consumer waste.

*Library of Congress Cataloging-in-Publication Data*
Whiting, Jim, 1943–
  A new generation of warriors: the history of mixed martial arts / by Jim Whiting.
    p. cm. — (Velocity — the world of mixed martial arts)
  Includes bibliographical references and index.
  Summary: "Discusses the history behind mixed martial arts as well as the sport's dark days and its current popularity" — Provided by publisher.
    ISBN 978-1-4296-3427-4 (library binding)
    1. Mixed martial arts — History — Juvenile literature. I. Title. II. Series.
  GV1102.7.M59W55 2010
  796.8 — dc22                                                    2009007339


Editorial Credits
Abby Czeskleba, editor; Kyle Grenz, designer; Eric Gohl, media researcher

Photo Credits
BigStockPhoto.com/Andrei Moldovan, 24–25; The Bridgeman Art Library/Look and Learn/ Private Collection, 14; Capstone Press/Karon Dubke, 12–13, 15; Cartesia, 12 (China map), 14 (Japan map), 35 (U.S. map); Comstock Images, 10; CORBIS/Sygma/Evan Hurd, 32–33; Courtesy of Rorion Gracie/Gracie Jiu-Jitsu Academy, 19, 20, 21, 22–23, 23, 26; Digital Vision, 16; Getty Images Inc./Allsport/Markus Boesch, 28–29; Getty Images Inc./ Claire Greenway, 38–39; Getty Images Inc./Jon Kopaloff, cover, 42–43; iStockphoto/ Gerville Hall, 40 (money, gloves); Landov LLC/Reuters/Tiffany Brown, 44–45; Mary Evans Picture Library, 6–7; Mary Evans Picture Library/Douglas McCarthy, 5; Matt Bruning 36–37 (illustrations); Newscom/Icon SMI/Zuma/Kevin Lock, 30; Newscom/Splash News and Pictures/Ray Nichols, 31; Shutterstock/Alexander Ishchenko, 8, 9; Shutterstock/Anton Novik, 35 (TV); Shutterstock/Dianna Toney, 4; Shutterstock/Frontpage, 34 (McCain); Shutterstock/keellla (chain link, throughout); Shutterstock/Piotr Sikora, 17; Shutterstock/S. Borisov, 34–35 (U.S. Capitol); Wikimedia/East718, 40 (belt); Wikimedia/public domain, 18


Capstone Press thanks Rorion Gracie of *www.gracieacademy.com* for donating the Gracie family photos used in this book.

The Unified Rules of Mixed Martial Arts on pages 36–37 can be found at:
*www.ufc.com/index.cfm?fa=LearnUFC.Rules*

# TABLE OF CONTENTS

# THE FIRST COMPETITIONS

Imagine an ancient battle scene with enemy soldiers rushing toward each other. Clashing weapons can be heard over the sound of injured soldiers screaming in pain. This scene may not be common today, but it certainly was thousands of years ago.

During ancient times, soldiers attacked their enemies with swords, spears, and knives. But these weapons often broke when they clanged against shields, armor, and other weapons. Sometimes weapons slipped from soldiers' blood-drenched hands. Without weapons, soldiers had no choice but to defend themselves with their bare hands.

When soldiers weren't fighting in battles, they spent time training. Soldiers held contests to see which man had the best skills.

**FACT:** The ancient Olympics began in 776 BC and lasted more than 1,000 years. The Olympics we know today started in 1896.

4

These early contests developed into sports and athletic festivals. The most famous of these festivals was the ancient Olympic Games.

The Olympics were held every four years in the Greek village of Olympia. Events included running, boxing, and wrestling. But the fans' favorite sport was an early version of mixed martial arts (MMA) called **pankration**.

Because pankration had so few rules, broken bones and other serious injuries were common. It was not unheard of for a fighter to die during a pankration match.

Thankfully, there are more rules to protect MMA fighters today than there were for pankration. MMA has emerged from pankration's violent roots to become one of the most popular sports in the United States. That's saying a lot for a sport that wasn't expected to survive its dark days in the 1990s.

**pankration** — an ancient fighting style that uses wrestling and boxing moves

It was the Olympic Games of 564 BC. Arrichion, the two-time defending pankration champion, was in serious trouble. His opponent jumped on Arrichion's back, wrapped his legs around Arrichion's waist, and began choking him.

While the opponent's moves were brutal, they were not against the rules. Pankratiasts could not bite an opponent or gouge his eyes. Everything else was legal. In fact, one pankratiast was known for breaking his opponents' fingers at the beginning of matches. He was nicknamed "Mr. Fingertips."

**FACT:** Pankration became part of the Olympics in 648 BC.

To counter his opponent's move, Arrichion used his leg to hook his opponent's foot. Arrichion then fell backward. The sudden move surprised the opponent. He screamed in pain as his ankle snapped. He raised his hand to signal his defeat. The fight was over.

When the judges went to congratulate Arrichion, he was dead. It was the first time in Olympic history that a dead person was awarded the victory wreath.

Although Arrichion was a pankratiast, he practiced many of the skills used in ancient wrestling and boxing. Pankration was developed from these two sports.

Many people believe wrestling is the world's oldest sport. It joined the first Olympics in 776 BC. In ancient wrestling, the first person to score three falls against an opponent became the winner. In order for the fall to count, the wrestler had to pin his opponent's hip, shoulder, or back against the ground.

When the Olympics began again in 1896 after more than a 1,000-year break, wrestling had changed. The first type, called Greco-Roman wrestling, was seen at the first modern Olympics in 1896. The two Greco-Roman wrestlers duked it out in a sandpit. Freestyle wrestling was added to the 1904 Olympic Games.

**FACT:** Like pankratiasts, wrestlers from ancient times were allowed to break opponents' fingers.

## GRECO-ROMAN WRESTLING

Greco-Roman wrestlers attack each other with their arms and upper bodies. These wrestlers can't use holds below an opponent's waist. They also can't use their legs to trip or hold an opponent. A wrestler who wraps his legs around a downed opponent will instantly lose the match.

# FREESTYLE WRESTLING

When it comes to comparing styles, freestyle wrestlers have fewer rules to follow than Greco-Roman competitors. Freestyle wrestlers use their entire bodies during a match. They use their legs to push, trip, and lift opponents. A wrestler can attack almost any part of his opponent's body. Holds above and below the waist are also allowed.

**FACT:** American Henry Cejudo won the gold medal in freestyle 55-kilogram wrestling at the 2008 Olympic Games. Cejudo competed in only one world tournament before the Olympics.

In both styles, a wrestler tries to pin an opponent's shoulders to the mat. If there is no pin, the wrestler who scores more points wins the match.

# ANCIENT BOXING

Boxing was introduced to the Olympics in 688 BC. Fights had no rounds or weight classes. To strengthen their wrists and fingers, boxers wrapped leather straps around their hands. The straps also protected the knuckles. Boxers originally used soft leather. They soon switched to hard leather straps because these straps caused more damage to opponents.

During ancient times, boxers tried to knock out their opponents. If boxers weren't knocked out, they raised a hand to admit defeat and end the match.

# MODERN BOXING

Today, boxing matches have rounds and weight classes. Just like ancient boxers, today's boxers win by knocking out their opponents. If a knockout doesn't happen, judges decide the winner at the end of the match.

*Boxing gloves weigh 8 to 10 ounces (227 to 283 grams).*

10

Dioxippus of Athens was one of the most famous ancient Greek pankratiasts. He automatically won the Olympic pankration championship in 336 BC because no one was willing to fight him.

Legend has it that Coragus, a Macedonian, challenged Dioxippus, a Greek, to a duel. The Macedonians and Greeks were enemies. As a soldier in Alexander the Great's army, Coragus had fought battles before. It appeared he was not afraid of Dioxippus.

The day of the battle, Coragus dressed in full armor and carried a javelin, spear, and sword. Dioxippus carried a small club. He did not wear armor to protect his body.

One by one, Coragus lost his weapons. First, Dioxippus dodged the javelin. Then Coragus rushed forward with his spear. Dioxippus smashed the spear with his club. When Coragus tried to draw his sword, Dioxippus tripped him. After hurling Coragus to the ground, Dioxippus put his foot on Coragus' neck and forced him to admit defeat.

Alexander was embarrassed that one of his best fighters had lost the duel. He falsely accused Dioxippus of theft. Dioxippus killed himself because he thought no one would ever believe he was innocent.

# CHAMPIONSHIP BELTS

Ask any boxer, and he'll tell you his number one goal is to win a championship belt. But sometimes one belt isn't enough. Boxers can earn more than one championship belt within their weight class.

Four primary boxing organizations put on professional fights. There are 17 weight classes in each organization, which means a boxer can win up to four belts in one weight class.

## PRIMARY BOXING ORGANIZATIONS

International Boxing Federation (IBF)

World Boxing Association (WBA)

World Boxing Council (WBC)

World Boxing Organization (WBO)

# THE MARTIAL ARTS OF MMA

There's no doubt that pankration, wrestling, and boxing have made MMA what it is today. But there's more to MMA history than just sports. Modern MMA fighters also use martial arts moves to throw an opponent off guard.

Many martial arts began in China as combat training for soldiers. Martial arts later spread throughout Asia. Jiu-jitsu, karate, Muay Thai, kickboxing, and judo are just some of the martial arts that affected MMA's development.

12

Jiu-jitsu began several centuries ago in Japan. The martial art helped men defend themselves by using their bare hands. The men's opponents often fought with weapons.

A jiu-jitsu fighter's punches were useless against an opponent's weapons and armor. Fighters waited for their enemies to attack. Jiu-jitsu fighters then used their opponents' weight to throw them to the ground. Jiu-jitsu fighters choked their downed opponents to keep them from moving.

Today's jiu-jitsu fighters still use chokes. Pins, joint locks, and punches also help to weaken opponents. The best jiu-jitsu fighters use an opponent's energy against him.

# KARATE

The early days of karate can be traced back to the Ryukyu Islands. Today one of the islands is better known as Okinawa. Japanese soldiers called samurai took over modern-day Okinawa in the early 1600s.

The people of Okinawa learned karate to defend themselves because the samurai took away their weapons. The people used their hands, elbows, and feet to fight the samurai.

**FACT:** Karate means "empty hands."

Japanese soldiers began using karate moves in the early 1900s. Karate became even more popular in Japan after the 1920s.

These days, karate focuses on striking as well as attacking an opponent's joints and other areas.

# MUAY THAI & KICKBOXING

Muay Thai began on battlefields hundreds of years ago. Soldiers were trained in Krabi Krabong. They used weapons as part of their training. But the soldiers had to learn to defend themselves without weapons. Soldiers used more than just their hands to attack their enemies.

Many people believe kickboxing is a combination of Muay Thai and karate.

Muay Thai fighters and kickboxers use their legs, knees, feet, elbows, and fists to hurt opponents. For this reason, Muay Thai is known as the art of eight limbs.

FACT: Muay Thai is also called Thai boxing.

# JUDO

In the late 1800s, Jigoro Kano used his knowledge of jiu-jitsu to develop judo. Judo fighters learn how to use an opponent's weight against him. Because judo fighters cannot punch or kick each other, they use throws, chokeholds, joint locks, and takedowns. Judo became a way for smaller fighters to defeat much larger opponents. To increase the popularity of judo, Kano taught his new sport to students.

A student named Mitsuyo Maeda would soon travel the world using his jiu-jitsu and judo skills in competitions. Not only would Maeda carry on Kano's **legacy**, but Maeda's teachings would lead another man, Helio Gracie, to start his own legacy.

# in BRAZIL, ANYTHING GOES

Maeda went to Brazil in 1915 and met Gastão Gracie. Gracie helped him find a place to live. The grateful Maeda taught jiu-jitsu to Gracie's oldest son, Carlos.

*Jigoro Kano taught jiu-jitsu and judo.*

Maeda was strong and powerful even though he stood just 5 feet, 5 inches (1.7 meters) tall and weighed only 155 pounds (70 kilograms).

Carlos then taught the art to all but one of his brothers. His youngest brother, Helio, was too weak to practice jiu-jitsu.

# THE BEGINNING OF BRAZILIAN JIU-JITSU

The Gracie brothers moved to Rio de Janeiro, Brazil, where Carlos opened the Gracie Jiu-Jitsu Academy.

*Carlos practiced jiu-jitsu for most of his life after learning the art from Mitsuyo Maeda.*

Helio often watched Carlos teach lessons. Helio learned jiu-jitsu by watching Carlos.

One day, Carlos didn't show up to teach a private lesson. Sixteen-year-old Helio offered to take his brother's place. Helio did such a good job that the student asked him to be his teacher.

When Helio started practicing jiu-jitsu with other people, his opponents often flung him to the mat. He developed a new system to fight back.

Jiu-jitsu focuses on upper-arm strength. Because of his weak body, Helio found that jiu-jitsu moves were difficult to execute. Rather than using judo and jiu-jitsu throws, Helio focused on ground fighting.

Helio used his legs to control his opponents in the guard position. While in the guard, he wrapped his legs around the other fighter.

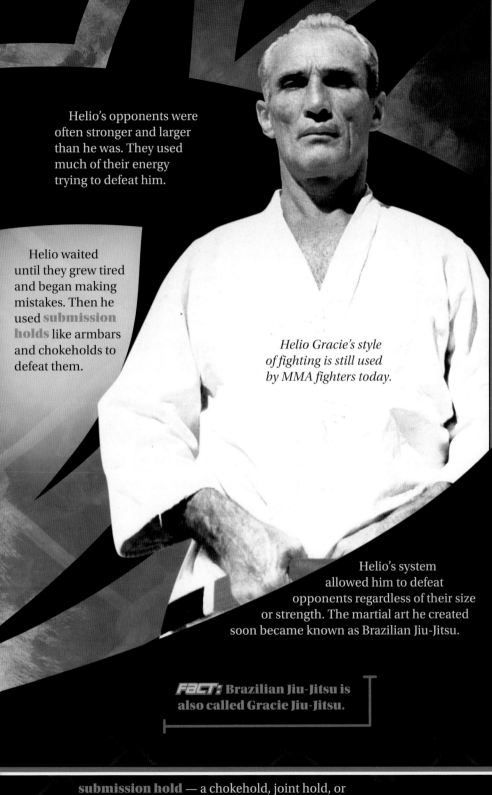

Helio's opponents were often stronger and larger than he was. They used much of their energy trying to defeat him.

Helio waited until they grew tired and began making mistakes. Then he used **submission holds** like armbars and chokeholds to defeat them.

*Helio Gracie's style of fighting is still used by MMA fighters today.*

Helio's system allowed him to defeat opponents regardless of their size or strength. The martial art he created soon became known as Brazilian Jiu-Jitsu.

**FACT:** Brazilian Jiu-Jitsu is also called Gracie Jiu-Jitsu.

**submission hold** — a chokehold, joint hold, or compression lock that causes a fighter's opponent to end the match by tapping out or saying, "I submit."

# NO-HOLDS-BARRED

At age 17, Helio began fighting in no-holds-barred matches. His fights became so popular that they were held in soccer stadiums. Fans loved watching Helio defeat opponents who outweighed him. No-holds-barred matches became one of the most popular spectator sports in Brazil.

*Brothers Carlos and Helio Gracie practiced different styles of jiu-jitsu.*

**FACT:** In Brazil, no-holds-barred matches are called *vale tudo. Vale tudo* means "anything goes" in Portuguese.

no-holds-barred — a fighting style in which all strikes are legal for fighters to use on one another

22

When he was 50, Helio fought a former student named Valdemar Santana. Santana was much younger and larger than Gracie. The match lasted for almost four hours. It finally ended when Santana kicked Helio in the head. Helio fell to the mat. He didn't have enough energy to continue fighting. The match was over.

Helio's fighting career continued for more than three decades. He passed on Brazilian Jiu-Jitsu to his seven sons. One of them took his father's skills and helped the sport's popularity grow.

CHAPTER

# 4 COMING TO THE UNITED STATES

Rorion Gracie, Helio's oldest son, moved to the United States in 1978. He wanted to bring his father's art to the United States. Rorion set up a training studio in the garage of his home in California. But he had a difficult time convincing people to take up the sport.

*Today, people around the world practice Brazilian Jiu-Jitsu.*

Rorion wasn't discouraged even though he only had a handful of students. He kept trying to interest people in Brazilian Jiu-Jitsu. In addition to giving lessons, he made several videos of his family in action.

# RORION'S BIG BREAK

In 1989, Rorion finally got the attention he wanted. A writer heard about his fighting ability and wrote a magazine article. The article called Rorion "the toughest man in the United States."

An advertising executive named Art Davie read the article. He began taking lessons with Gracie. Soon the two men became partners and worked together to promote Gracie's videos.

Rorion had fond memories of watching no-holds-barred matches on TV when he lived in Brazil.

Rorion and Davie came up with the idea for a TV show that would pit different fighting styles against one another. Was karate better than jiu-jitsu? How did boxing and wrestling measure up to each other? Rorion and Art Davie wanted to find out.

The show, called *War of the Worlds*, would appear on **pay-per-view** (PPV). The money from live audiences and PPV would help produce the show.

Rorion and Davie kept knocking on doors until Semaphore Entertainment Group (SEG) agreed to work with them. The company was looking for new PPV events. The show would be the first of its kind.

**FACT:** The creators of *War of the Worlds* gave the show its name because they thought every martial art was its own world.

**pay-per-view** — a service for cable TV viewers in which customers order and view a single movie or televised event for a fee

# DESIGNING THE CAGE

Because organizers didn't want one fighting style to have an advantage over another, they created the Octagon. This new eight-sided arena was surrounded by padded fencing that kept fighters from falling out and hurting themselves.

## UFC 1

SEG soon changed the show's name to the Ultimate Fighting Championship (UFC). The UFC held its first event in Denver, Colorado, on November 12, 1993. The winner would be crowned the Ultimate Fighter. His fighting style would be king of the MMA world.

*Kickboxer Kevin Rosier won his match against karate expert Zane Frazier at UFC 1.*

To attract fans, the event was advertised as no-holds-barred. But that wasn't completely true. There were rules against biting and eye gouging.

Eight men competed in one-on-one matches at UFC 1. The winner of each fight moved to the next round. The last two fighters squared off for the championship and a $50,000 prize.

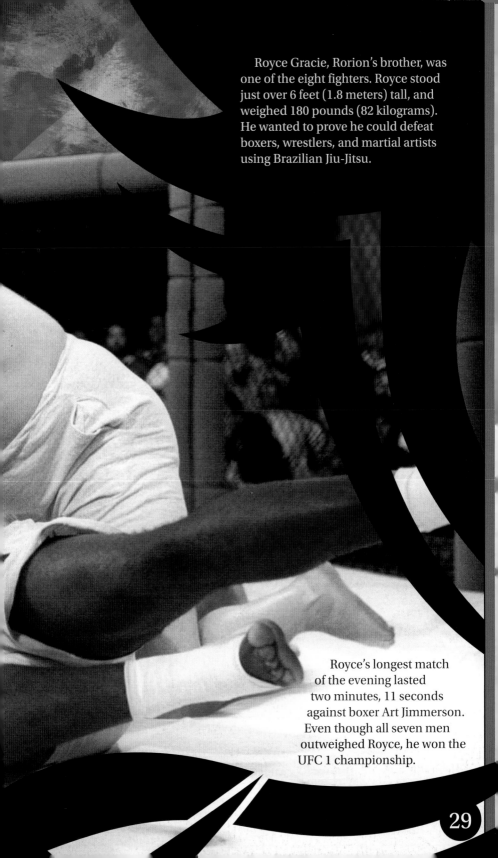

Royce Gracie, Rorion's brother, was one of the eight fighters. Royce stood just over 6 feet (1.8 meters) tall, and weighed 180 pounds (82 kilograms). He wanted to prove he could defeat boxers, wrestlers, and martial artists using Brazilian Jiu-Jitsu.

Royce's longest match of the evening lasted two minutes, 11 seconds against boxer Art Jimmerson. Even though all seven men outweighed Royce, he won the UFC 1 championship.

Royce repeated his success four months later at UFC 2. This time there were 16 fighters, but the results were almost the same as UFC 1. Gracie won his first fight in five minutes, eight seconds. He took just over one minute to win each of his other three matches.

A third championship for Gracie looked promising after he beat Kimo Leopoldo in his first match at UFC 3. But Gracie's trainers threw in the towel before the second fight began. Gracie was dehydrated and too tired to compete. His second opponent, Harold Howard, earned a **technical knockout** (TKO) and moved to the next round.

Gracie

Determined to regain his championship, Royce returned to UFC 4 three months later. By then, fighters had started to learn Gracie's moves. He defeated his first opponent in less than three minutes, but his second fight took twice as long to finish. That was nothing compared to Royce's final-round match against Dan Severn.

The Gracie-Severn fight went on for more than 15 minutes. Gracie finally ended the grueling match with a submission hold to win the championship. While the live crowd witnessed the amazing ending, pay-per-view fans were not so lucky. TV viewers missed out on the final seconds of action. The PPV broadcast was cut off because the match lasted longer than UFC organizers expected.

Shamrock

A great deal of excitement surrounded UFC 5 in April 1995. Ken Shamrock, a fighter Gracie had defeated in UFC 1, had become a big name in the UFC.

FACT: From 1993 to 1995, Royce Gracie won 11 matches. His only loss during this time came at UFC 3 against Harold Howard.

# THE GRACIE-SHAMROCK REMATCH

Fans had been looking forward to a rematch between Gracie and Shamrock since UFC 1. To be sure the two men would meet in UFC 5, promoters added the Gracie-Shamrock "super fight" to the **fight card**.

The match had very little action. Hardly any punches were thrown and both men spent much of the time on the canvas. Fans began booing as the fight reached the halfway mark.

**fight card** — a list of matches during an MMA event

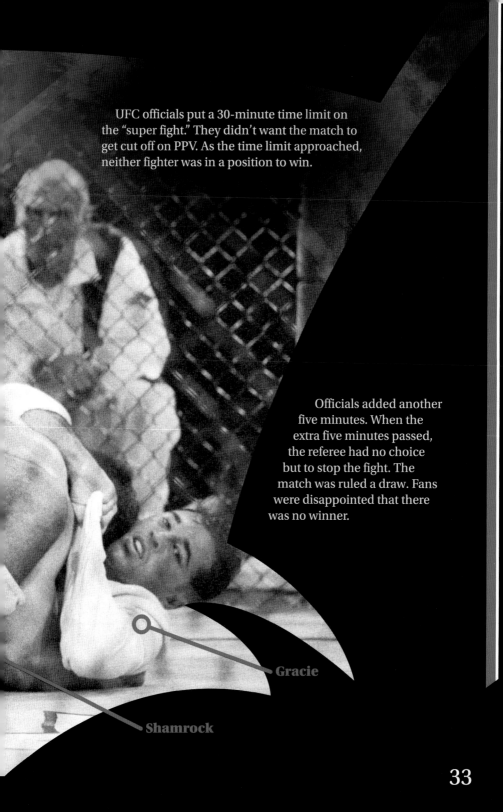

UFC officials put a 30-minute time limit on the "super fight." They didn't want the match to get cut off on PPV. As the time limit approached, neither fighter was in a position to win.

Officials added another five minutes. When the extra five minutes passed, the referee had no choice but to stop the fight. The match was ruled a draw. Fans were disappointed that there was no winner.

Gracie

Shamrock

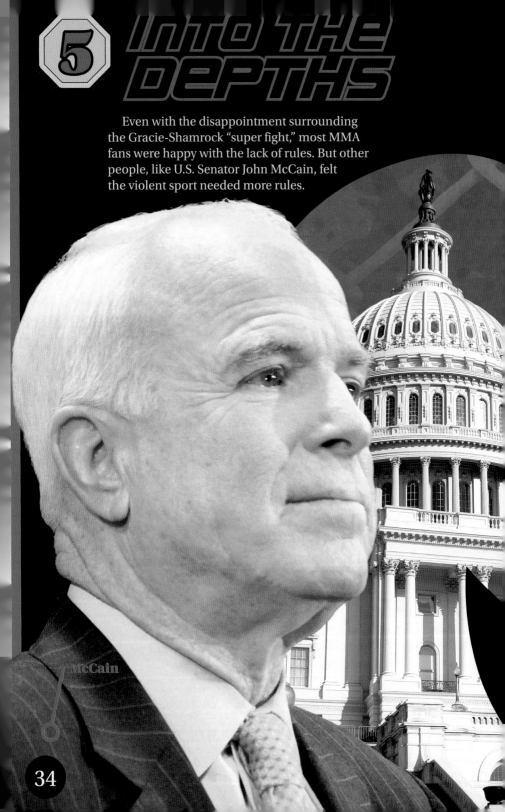

# 5 INTO THE DEPTHS

Even with the disappointment surrounding the Gracie-Shamrock "super fight," most MMA fans were happy with the lack of rules. But other people, like U.S. Senator John McCain, felt the violent sport needed more rules.

McCain

# McCAIN TAKES ACTION

In the mid-1990s, McCain urged the 50 state governors to ban MMA competitions. He also pressured major PPV broadcasters to stop televising MMA fights. It didn't take long for McCain's work to affect the sport.

It became increasingly difficult to find places where fights could be held. Sometimes fights took place in parking lots.

Other MMA fights were presented in night clubs with just a few hundred fans. All of the major PPV broadcasters stopped showing the fights on TV.

**FACT:** Many PPV providers stopped carrying UFC events after UFC 12 on February 8, 1997.

# SUCCESS IN JAPAN

MMA moved overseas when UFC began struggling in the United States. In 1997, a group of Japanese businessmen formed PRIDE Fighting Championships. More than 47,000 fans turned out for PRIDE 1 in Tokyo, Japan.

The event featured popular Japanese wrestler Nobuhiko Takada and Rickson Gracie. Gracie used an armbar near the end of the first round to win the match.

## MAKING THE RULES

The UFC had started to move away from its no-holds-barred fighting style. Fights now included judges and also had time limits.

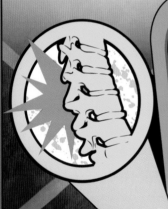

## UNIFIED RULES OF MIXED MARTIAL ARTS

The following actions are not allowed in MMA matches:

1. Head-butting
2. Eye gouging
3. Grabbing the collarbone
4. Hair pulling
5. Attacking an opponent on or during the break
6. Groin attacks
7. Putting a finger into any hole, cut, or wound on an opponent
8. Small-joint manipulation
9. Striking to the spine or the back of the head
10. Striking downward using the point of the elbow
11. Throat strikes of any kind, including grabbing the windpipe
12. Clawing, pinching, or twisting the flesh

The New Jersey State Athletic Control Board (NJSACB) helped to develop the Unified Rules of Mixed Martial Arts (URMMA). These rules were formally adopted by MMA organizations like the UFC in 2001. These rules established weight classes and spelled out 31 actions that were not allowed. These rules showed that fighter safety was important.

Many people believed it was only a matter of time before the sport would become popular again. But the years of struggle had cost the UFC a great deal of money. It was very possible that the organization would go out of business.

13. Biting
14. Kicking the head of a grounded opponent
15. Kneeing the head of a grounded opponent
16. Stomping a grounded opponent
17. Kicking the kidney with the heel
18. Spiking an opponent to the canvas on his head or neck
19. Throwing an opponent out of the ring or fenced area
20. Holding the shorts or gloves of an opponent
21. Spitting at an opponent
22. Engaging in unsportsmanlike conduct that injures an opponent
23. Holding the ropes or the fence
24. Using abusive language in the ring or fenced area

25. Fish hooking
26. Attacking an opponent who is under the care of the referee
27. Attacking an opponent after the bell has sounded the end of the period of unarmed combat
28. Ignoring the referee's instructions
29. Avoiding contact with an opponent, intentionally or consistently dropping the mouth guard, or faking an injury
30. Interference by the corner
31. Throwing in the towel during competition

# 6 THE COMEBACK

Semaphore Entertainment Group owners were tired of losing money. But convincing someone to buy a failing business was not an easy sell. Then SEG owners found one of the new owners in the strangest of places.

Back in 1999, SEG officials had begun focusing on Nevada. They wanted the Nevada State Athletic Commission to sanction MMA fights in the state. SEG representatives invited the commissioners to attend UFC 21 on July 16, 1999.

One of the commissioners was Las Vegas businessman Lorenzo Fertitta. He was very impressed with the fighters' training.

Frank Fertitta III

The other commissioners didn't share Fertitta's enthusiasm. SEG representatives realized there was no chance of getting permission to put on fights in Nevada.

SEG put the word out that they wanted a partner to share the cost of UFC events. Word quickly got back to Fertitta. He and his brother, Frank Fertitta III, formed Zuffa.

The Fertittas, along with Dana White, took over the UFC in 2001. The brothers made White the president of the UFC. White had managed and trained boxers and some MMA fighters. He later became a promoter.

**FACT:** Zuffa bought the UFC for $2 million.

Dana White

Lorenzo Fertitta

sanction — to approve an event and make it official

promoter — a person or company that puts on a sporting event

39

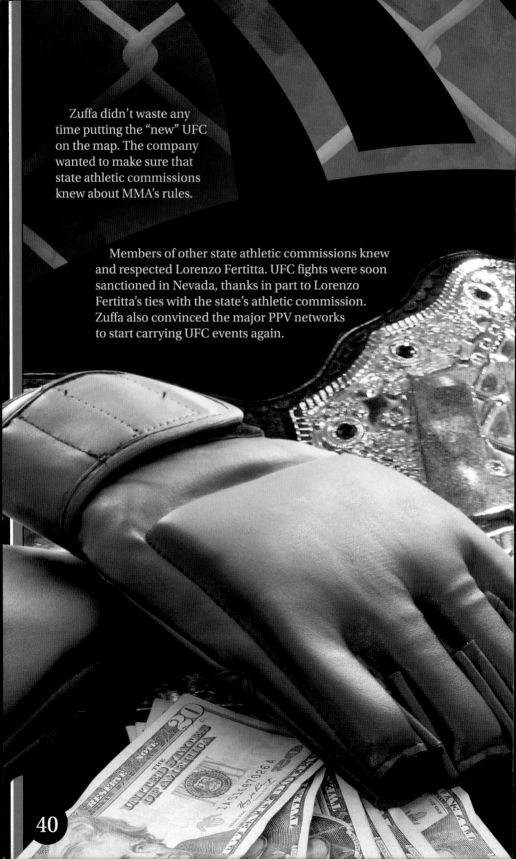

Zuffa didn't waste any time putting the "new" UFC on the map. The company wanted to make sure that state athletic commissions knew about MMA's rules.

Members of other state athletic commissions knew and respected Lorenzo Fertitta. UFC fights were soon sanctioned in Nevada, thanks in part to Lorenzo Fertitta's ties with the state's athletic commission. Zuffa also convinced the major PPV networks to start carrying UFC events again.

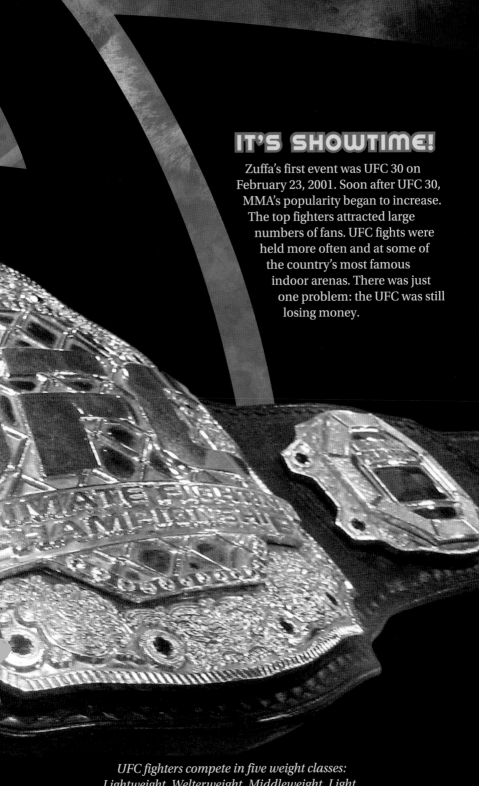

# IT'S SHOWTIME!

Zuffa's first event was UFC 30 on February 23, 2001. Soon after UFC 30, MMA's popularity began to increase. The top fighters attracted large numbers of fans. UFC fights were held more often and at some of the country's most famous indoor arenas. There was just one problem: the UFC was still losing money.

*UFC fighters compete in five weight classes: Lightweight, Welterweight, Middleweight, Light Heavyweight, and Heavyweight. Each weight class has its own championship belt.*

# THE ULTIMATE FIGHTER

The Fertittas had an idea for an MMA reality show. The show, called *The Ultimate Fighter*, would help the UFC earn money. Reality TV shows like *Survivor* and *American Idol* were drawing millions of viewers. The Fertittas hoped *The Ultimate Fighter* would do the same.

As the Fertittas approached different TV networks, they found that no one was interested. Finally the brothers approached Spike TV, a cable network with shows geared toward young men. Zuffa offered to pay the show's production costs. Spike snapped up *The Ultimate Fighter*.

The show began in January 2005. A group of 16 up-and-coming fighters competed for a chance at a UFC contract. They trained with UFC stars Randy Couture and Chuck Liddell. Two fighters squared off in a fight each week. The loser had to leave the show.

*The Ultimate Fighter* helped put the UFC on the map. People who had never seen an MMA match were now tuning in to watch their favorite fighters every week.

# GRIFFIN VS. BONNAR

The final night of *The Ultimate Fighter* featured a fight between light heavyweights Forrest Griffin and Stephan Bonnar. The Griffin-Bonnar fight is considered one of the best matches in UFC history. Both men slugged it out for the full three rounds. Griffin won the match by **unanimous decision**. The match was so close that Dana White awarded both fighters UFC contracts.

The event jumpstarted Griffin's career. He became one of the coaches for *The Ultimate Fighter* in 2008. Later that year, he defeated Quinton Jackson to become the UFC light-heavyweight champion.

The Griffin-Bonnar fight introduced MMA to many people. The audience for UFC fights would soon be as large as championship boxing matches.

As UFC increased in popularity, a number of other MMA promotions like HDNet Fights and World Extreme Cagefighting developed. The growing number of promotions proved that the interest in MMA had grown.

44

# ELITE XTREME COMBAT
## (Elite XC)

On May 31, 2008, an MMA promotion called Elite XC made history. It was on this night that the CBS network broadcast its first Elite XC event. Elite XC was the first time a live MMA event appeared on network TV.

The Elite XC event was also the first time that many viewers had seen women compete. Female fighters don't spend much time in the MMA spotlight because the sport's largest promotion, the UFC, does not allow females to compete.

Fans expected the main event between Kimbo Slice and James Thompson to be the best fight of the evening. But the fight between Gina Carano and Kaitlin Young stole the show.

Elite XC went on to televise two more events with CBS, but the promotion went out of business in October 2008. One reason the promotion failed was because TV viewers didn't have to pay PPV fees. However, fans will not forget how the promotion increased MMA's popularity.

MMA has come a long way since its dark days in the 1990s. There's no telling what the future holds for MMA. But one thing is for sure: the sport's hard-hitting punches and jaw-dropping kicks will keep fans on their feet for generations to come.

unanimous decision — a situation in which all three judges agree on a winner

# GLOSSARY

**brutal** (BROO-tuhl) — cruel and violent

**dehydrated** (dee-HY-dray-tuhd) — not having enough water

**fight card** (FITE KARD) — a list of matches during an MMA event

**legacy** (LEG-uh-see) — something handed down from one generation to another

**no-holds-barred** (NOH HOHLDS BARD) — a fighting style in which all strikes are legal for fighters to use on one another; MMA fights are no longer no-holds-barred.

**pankration** (pan-KRAY-shuhn) — an ancient fighting style that uses wrestling and boxing moves

**pay-per-view** (PAY PUR VYOO) — a service for cable TV viewers in which customers order and view a single movie or televised event for a fee

**promoter** (pruh-MOH-tur) — a person or company that puts on a sporting event

**sanction** (SANGK-shuhn) — to approve an event and make it official

**submission hold** (suhb-MISH-uhn HOHLD) — a chokehold, joint hold, or compression lock that causes a fighter's opponent to end the match by tapping out or saying, "I submit."

**survive** (sur-VIVE) — to continue to live or exist

**technical knockout** (TEK-nuh-kuhl NOK-out) — the act of stopping a fight when a fighter is at risk of serious injury if the fight continues

**unanimous decision** (yoo-NAN-uh-muhss di-SIZH-uhn) — a situation in which all three judges agree on a winner

# read more

Franklin, Rich, and Jon F. Merz. *The Complete Idiot's Guide to Ultimate Fighting.* Indianapolis: Alpha, 2007.

Ollhoff, Jim. *Martial Arts Around the Globe.* The World of Martial Arts. Edina, Minn.: ABDO, 2008.

Ollhoff, Jim. *Martial Arts Movies.* The World of Martial Arts. Edina, Minn.: ABDO, 2008.

Shamrock, Frank. *Mixed Martial Arts for Dummies.* Indianapolis: Wiley, 2009.

# INTERNET SITES

FactHound offers a safe, fun way to find Internet sites related to this book. All of the sites on FactHound have been researched by our staff.

Here's all you do:

Visit *www.facthound.com*

FactHound will fetch the best sites for you!